Zoe's Rescue Zoo

The Adventurous Arctic Fox

Amelia Cobb

Illustrated by
Sophy Williams

nosy
crow

With special thanks to Siobhan Curham

For the fantastic kids of E. Franklin Street

First published in the UK in 2022 by Nosy Crow Ltd
The Crow's Nest, 14 Baden Place
Crosby Row, London SE1 1YW, UK

Nosy Crow Eireann Ltd
44 Orchard Grove, Kenmare
Co Kerry, V93 FY22, Ireland

Nosy Crow and associated logos are trademarks and/or
registered trademarks of Nosy Crow Ltd

Text copyright © Working Partners Ltd, 2022
Illustrations © Sophy Williams, 2022

The right of Working Partners Ltd and Sophy Williams to be identified as the author
and illustrator respectively of this work has been asserted by them in accordance with the
Copyright, Designs and Patents Act 1988.

ISBN: 978 1 83994 561 8

A CIP catalogue record for this book will be available from the British Library

Printed and bound in Great Britain by Clays Ltd, Elcograf S.p.A.

Papers used by Nosy Crow are made from wood grown in sustainable forests.

1 3 5 7 9 10 8 6 4 2

www.nosycrow.com

Chapter One
The Beard with Eyes!

Zoe Parker smiled as she brushed away some snowflakes from a sparkly red bauble and pinned it to the fence. It was almost Christmas. Many of her friends would be decorating their homes, but she was pretty sure she was the only one decorating a red panda's enclosure!

Ruby the red panda scampered

down from a tree and waved her paws, squeaking loudly.

"I'm glad you like the decoration, Ruby," said Zoe. "I chose the red one especially for you because it's the same colour as your fur!"

Zoe had a very special secret. She could understand what animals were saying and talk to them! And there were lots of animals to talk to, because Zoe lived at the Rescue Zoo! The zoo belonged to her Great-Uncle Horace, a world-famous explorer and animal expert. He had created the zoo as a safe place for animals to come and stay if they were endangered, lost or hurt. Zoe lived in a cosy cottage at the edge of the zoo with her mum, Lucy, who was the zoo's vet.

"Can I have a silver bauble to match

my fur?" asked Meep, climbing out of Zoe's basket of decorations and on to her shoulder. "I'd like to be sparkly for Christmas!"

"But you're already sparkly, Meep!" giggled Zoe. The grey mouse lemur's fur was covered in red glitter from her basket, and Zoe gently brushed some of it away.

Meep wriggled and chirped happily. The little creature was Zoe's best friend, and he lived in the cottage with her too! He was very small with a long curling tail and soft ears that stuck up in the air.

Just then, they heard the sound of shoes crunching on the footpath.

"Uh-oh!" exclaimed Meep, and he quickly hid in Zoe's fur-lined hood. Zoe's heart sank. There was only one person who marched around like that – Mr Pinch, the grumpy zoo manager.

"What on earth are you doing?" asked Mr Pinch crossly, staring at the red bauble.

"I'm decorating Ruby's enclosure," replied Zoe. "We're making the zoo look pretty for the special Christmas event in a few days. When visitors come to watch all the animals get their Christmas treats, the zoo should look extra special." She pointed to the penguin enclosure, where her mum and some of the zookeepers were hanging a string of fairy lights.

"But why have you hung a red bauble next to the silver ones?" grumbled Mr Pinch, pointing to the other baubles tied to the fence. "They should all be the same colour."

"Why?" said Zoe.

"Because having one colour looks neater, of course," Mr Pinch huffed.

Zoe sighed. Mr Pinch was always complaining that the zoo didn't look tidy enough. A few more flakes of snow drifted down from the sky.

"Oh no! Oh no!" spluttered Mr Pinch.

"What's wrong?" asked Zoe.

"It's snowing even harder than before!"

"But that's good. It will make the zoo look even more Christmassy," Zoe pointed out.

"It will make it look Christ-*messy*, more like!" Mr Pinch marched off, muttering under his breath.

"Is it safe?" asked Meep, popping his head out from Zoe's hood.

"Yes, don't worry, he's gone," giggled Zoe.

"Good!" chirped Meep.

Zoe turned back to the fence. "Now, I wonder if we should decorate the empty enclosure next to Ruby's." With its grey rocks and muddy ground, the enclosure looked dull and dreary next to the others. "Let's go and ask Mum."

Zoe set off to the penguin enclosure, with Meep riding on her shoulder. When they got there, they found Zoe's mum, Lucy, and Ethan, the wolf keeper, busy writing a list.

"Hello, Mum, what are you writing?" asked Zoe.

"A list of all the delicious Christmas treats we're going to give the animals." Lucy smiled.

"We're going to gift wrap them," added Ethan.

"What are the mouse lemurs getting?" cheeped Meep in Zoe's ear.

"What treats are the herbivores getting, Mum?" asked Zoe.

"We were wondering if you could come up with an idea for them," replied Lucy.

"I'd like a bunch of bananas and a box of berries, and some nuts would be nice, and maybe some leaves," chattered Meep.

Zoe pulled up her scarf to hide her smile. Food was definitely Meep's favourite subject. She pretended to think about an answer to her mother's question before saying, "Maybe we could make them Christmas wreathes from their favourite nuts and berries and plants."

"What a lovely idea," said Ethan.

"May I have my Christmas wreath now?" Meep chirped with excitement.

"Not yet, but I promise to give you a treat later," whispered Zoe, careful that Ethan and Lucy didn't hear.

Zoe spotted some of her penguin friends by the enclosure wall and went over to visit them. The huge iceberg at the centre of their lagoon looked even better with a dusting of real snow. Another flurry of snowflakes tumbled through the air and the penguins clapped their wings with glee.

"Yes, it's lovely to see the snow," agreed Zoe.

Meep hopped down from her shoulder and waved his tiny paws at the sky.

"Are you happy to see the snow too?" asked Zoe.

Meep shook his head. "Goo! Goo!" he cried. It was Meep's nickname for a very special person that Zoe was always excited to see!

Zoe stared up into the sky and spotted a bright splash of colour drifting down between the snowflakes. Yes! It was Great-Uncle Horace's hot-air balloon, and it was coming in to land.

"Look!" cried Zoe, running back to Lucy and Ethan. "It's Great-Uncle Horace! He must have rescued a new animal."

"I wonder what it could be this time," said Lucy as the balloon drifted closer and closer.

They raced to a clearing near the front

of the zoo and watched the balloon come down with a bump. Great-Uncle Horace stood in the basket of the balloon. He had a beaming smile on his face and his beautiful hyacinth macaw, Kiki, perched on his shoulder.

A crowd of zookeepers gathered around the balloon, waving to Great-Uncle Horace and Kiki.

"Greetings, everyone!" Great-Uncle Horace boomed. His white beard was longer and bushier than ever and seemed to wrap around his neck. As he spoke, his beard began twitching from side to side.

Meep jumped up and down with excitement.

"What is it?" whispered Zoe, picking him up.

"Goo's beard is alive!" chattered the little mouse lemur. "Goo's beard has eyes!"

Zoe looked back at Great-Uncle Horace. To her surprise, his beard began shaking more vigorously and a pair of bright-blue eyes blinked out at her.

Meep chattered and waved his paws.

A fluffy white tail flicked out from beneath Great-Uncle Horace's beard and a pointy white face appeared by his chin. Zoe stared in amazement.

"How wonderful to see you, Zoe! And Meep too!" said Great-Uncle Horace with a twinkly-eyed grin. "I see you've spotted our newest arrival."

"Hello, Great-Uncle Horace!" cried
Zoe. "Who have you rescued this time?"

Great-Uncle Horace scooped the
fluffy white animal into his hands and
it yapped happily. "This is Indie," he
replied. "She's an Arctic fox."

Chapter Two
Indie the Adventurer

As Great-Uncle Horace got out of the balloon, the little Arctic fox scampered around, sniffing Zoe, Lucy and Ethan curiously.

"Why is she called Indie?" asked Zoe.

"She's named after a character in an old adventure movie," replied Great-Uncle Horace. "She was given the name because she's so brave and curious and loves an adventure, as you can see." He chuckled as Indie leapt on to the rim of the balloon basket.

"Did you rescue her from the Arctic?" asked Zoe.

"No. She's from another zoo that has more foxes than they can take care of. Indie was so adventurous that the other zookeepers felt she needed her own special space to explore. So they gave her to us."

Indie hopped down from the basket and scampered over to Zoe, nuzzling against her legs.

"She's so soft and fluffy!" exclaimed Zoe as she bent down to stroke her.

"She needs to be," replied Great-Uncle Horace. "It gets *very* cold in the Arctic."

"That's why her tail is so long and bushy," said Ethan. "She can use it to help her keep warm, like a scarf. She's a beautiful animal!"

"I wish I had a fluffy scarf attached to me." Meep shivered as a snowflake landed on the tip of his nose. Mouse lemurs were from Madagascar, a very hot country, so he didn't like the cold. Zoe opened the top of her coat a little bit so that Meep could climb in and share her warmth. His little face poked out over the top of the zip.

"They have fur on the bottom of their

paws too," continued Ethan. "It stops their feet from getting frostbite. It's like they're wearing fluffy slippers."

Zoe smiled. She had a pair of fluffy penguin slippers. They kept her feet lovely and warm in the winter.

"Would you like to help me get Indie settled into her new enclosure, Zoe?" asked Great-Uncle Horace.

"Yes please!" replied Zoe. She wanted to be a zookeeper when she grew up, so she always loved to help with the animals.

"We're going to put her in the empty enclosure next to Ruby's," said Great-Uncle Horace.

"She'll be really happy there," said Ethan as they walked over to the enclosure.

"Are you sure?"
Zoe looked at the
drab enclosure. She
wished she'd had time to decorate it.

"Absolutely," Great-Uncle Horace
said. "Arctic foxes love rocks to climb
and ground to dig burrows in. They're
excellent at burrowing."

Zoe opened the enclosure gate using a
paw-shaped pendant that hung around
her neck. The pendant had been a
gift from Great-Uncle Horace and it
opened every enclosure in the zoo. The
zookeepers used pass-cards to get into the

enclosures, but Zoe's necklace was one of a kind.

In her enclosure next door, Ruby clambered up a tree and watched the new arrival curiously. Indie went racing past Zoe into her enclosure, sniffing at the bushes. Then she scampered up the rocks, which were now covered in a thin layer of snow.

"It's hard to see her in the snow," laughed Zoe. "She's the same colour."

"Arctic foxes are great at camouflaging," explained Ethan.

"What does camouflaging mean?" Meep chattered beneath Zoe's chin.

"It's when something blends in with its surroundings," whispered Zoe. "Like Indie's fur and the snow."

"And Goo's beard!" chirped Meep.

"Their coats are white during the winter, but when the snow melts, their fur turns brownish-grey to match the rocks," continued Ethan.

"That's so cool," said Zoe.

"I wish I could camouflage," sighed Meep.

"Zoe, could you make our new arrival feel welcome while Ethan and I go and get her some food?" asked Great-Uncle Horace. "Keep an eye on her. She likes to explore!"

"Of course," replied Zoe.

As soon as the grown-ups had gone, Zoe crouched down beside Indie. "Hello," she said. "Welcome to the Rescue Zoo."

Indie gave her a cheery yelp, which made Zoe feel very relieved. Sometimes the new arrivals at the Rescue Zoo were sad or scared because they were feeling homesick, but Indie seemed really happy.

"I'm Zoe and this is Meep," continued Zoe. The little Arctic fox scampered around her, yapping happily. "Yes, I'm sure you'll have lots of adventures here," replied Zoe.

Indie nuzzled up against her and barked again, her whiskers twitching.

"I'm so glad you like your new

territory," replied Zoe. "And yes, there are some other animals nearby. Look, there's Ruby, she's a red panda." She pointed to the enclosure next door, where Ruby was running back and forth along the fence. Indie scampered over and both animals yapped at each other.

"Let's put some decorations up in Indie's enclosure," Zoe said to Meep, "and make it look more festive."

Just as they were hanging some sparkly gold and green baubles on the fence, a little boy and his parents came walking along the footpath.

"Look at that animal," the boy cried as soon as he saw Indie. "It looks like a fox that hasn't been coloured in!"

"Her name's Indie and she's an Arctic fox," explained Zoe. "Her fur is white so

she can blend in with the snow."

"Arctic foxes are cool," said the little
boy. "I think they're my new favourite
animal."

Indie scampered up and down in front
of the visitors, making the boy even more
excited.

"If we don't get a move on, we won't see any of the other animals," the boy's dad joked, and they set off along the path. Indie ran along the fence, following the visitors until she reached the end of her enclosure. Then she ran back to Zoe and started butting her leg with her pointy nose.

"What's she doing?" asked Meep as Indie began to squeak eagerly.

"She wants to go on an adventure with the humans," said Zoe. She bent down and patted Indie on the head. "I'm afraid you have to stay in your enclosure. But don't worry, there's lots to explore in there."

Just then Great-Uncle Horace and Ethan came back with a bowl of food for Indie.

26

"Great work with the decorations, Zoe," said Ethan.

"Speaking of decorations, your mum asked if you'd help her decorate the tree in the animal hospital," said Great-Uncle Horace.

"Sure, I'll be right there," Zoe agreed. She turned back to where Indie had been to say goodbye and frowned. The Arctic fox had disappeared!

"Where has Indie gone?" Meep chattered, poking his head out of Zoe's coat.

They heard a cheerful yap further up the path. Indie had escaped her enclosure!

"She really is an adventurous Arctic fox!" chuckled Ethan.

The little fox was barely visible against

the snow gathering on the ground. Zoe
listened carefully for her barking to find
her.

"There you are!" Zoe hurried to scoop Indie up and let her back into the enclosure using her special paw-print pendant. "Come on, Indie. Ethan and Great-Uncle Horace have brought you some food."

Ethan placed a bowl of meat on the ground for Indie.

When Zoe was sure the adults weren't listening, she crouched down so she could whisper in Indie's ear. "Don't worry, Indie, I'll be back soon and then we can plan some adventures."

By the time Zoe returned to see Indie, the zoo had shut for the night and it was almost dark. Flurries of snow swirled in the golden glow of the old-fashioned lamps lining the path.

"How's your new neighbour doing?" Zoe asked Ruby when she reached her enclosure.

Ruby squeaked happily and pointed a paw at the enclosure next door.

"Oh, look, Indie's made a new friend." Zoe picked Meep up so he could see into the enclosure. Indie was jumping out of holes in the ground and a magpie was flying above her, playfully squawking at her before fluttering out of reach. *I think Indie's going to fit in really well at the Rescue Zoo*, Zoe thought with a grin. Then she looked at Indie's fence and frowned. All of the gold baubles had disappeared!

Chapter Three
The Mystery of the Missing Baubles

The next morning, Zoe woke up bleary-eyed. She had lain awake for a long time, wondering what had happened to the golden baubles. With a groan, she made herself sit up and look out of the bedroom window.

"Yes!" she exclaimed, throwing back her blankets.

"What?" murmured Meep, who was still curled up on his cushion at the end of Zoe's bed.

"It's snowed even more in the night and the snow looks really thick."

"Really thick means really cold," said Meep with a shiver.

"Don't worry, I'll give you some extra food to help you stay warm," grinned Zoe.

"Extra food!" Meep bounded on to the floor. "Let's get going."

"All right, all right," laughed Zoe. "But after breakfast we must figure out what happened to the golden baubles!"

Downstairs in the kitchen, Lucy was making some pancake batter. "Oh, whoops!" she exclaimed, as she spilled flour on her jumper.

"You look like you've been out in the snow," joked Zoe. Lucy and Meep giggled.

"Great-Uncle Horace has asked if you can put up some more decorations after breakfast," said Lucy.

"After *extra* breakfast," squeaked Meep.

Trying really hard not to laugh, Zoe sliced a banana for Meep and added blueberries to his bowl too.

"I noticed some of the ones we already put up were missing last night," Zoe told Lucy.

"That's odd!" Lucy replied. "Maybe they fell off into the snow?"

"Maybe," Zoe agreed. "Wherever they are, Meep and I will find them."

Once they'd eaten, they set off through

the zoo. Zoe held a basket full of
decorations with Meep perched on top
of them, wearing a string of purple tinsel
like a scarf. The zoo hadn't opened to
visitors yet, and the thick blanket of
snow made everything seem peaceful and
still. As they passed the hippo enclosure,
Henry grunted a cheery greeting.

"Good morning, Henry. I like your tinsel," replied Zoe, pointing to the gold tinsel wrapped around the enclosure gate. Spying Mo, the hippo keeper, further along the enclosure, she hurried over.

"Hello, Zoe," called Mo. "Are you doing some more decorating?" He nodded at her basket.

"Yes. You didn't move any of the baubles by the new Arctic fox's enclosure, did you?"

He shook his head. "No, sorry."

Zoe asked every zookeeper the same question, but none of them knew where the gold baubles had gone.

When she reached Indie's enclosure she peered inside, but there was no sign of the little white fox. Zoe let herself in with her paw-print pendant and looked

35

around. The rocks and the ground were now covered with a thick carpet of snow. Meep shivered and hopped up into her warm furry hood.

"Good morning!" called Zoe, but there was still no sign of Indie.

"Where is she?" asked Meep.

"Maybe she's dug herself a burrow," replied Zoe. "Ethan said that Arctic foxes love to burrow."

She and Meep jumped as Indie suddenly appeared from the rocks. "Oh, you gave me a fright," gasped Zoe. "I didn't see you! You were so well camouflaged in the snow."

"I wish I could be camouflaged in the snow," chirped Meep.

"Yes, but think how cold you'd be," giggled Zoe.

As Indie rolled
around in the snow,
the magpie from the
day before swooped
down from
one of
the trees,
chattering
happily.

Indie flicked her tail at the bird and dived into a burrow. The magpie swooped down to a different part of the enclosure and chirped. The Arctic fox jumped out from another hole in the ground. Before Indie could catch the magpie, he fluttered out of reach and screeched playfully.

"Indie can't catch him," said Zoe.

Eventually the magpie flew to his tree to rest, but Indie was still full of energy. When she realised the magpie was no longer playing, the Arctic fox jumped out of her burrow again and scampered over to Zoe and Meep.

"Well done for making a new friend," said Zoe.

Indie barked.

"You want to have another adventure?" replied Zoe.

The little fox nodded and a sprinkling of powdery snowflakes fell from her fur.

"Why don't you explore your enclosure?" suggested Zoe.

Indie frowned and yelped.

"You've already explored it from top to bottom?" said Zoe.

Indie nodded and barked again.

"You want to have an adventure like you would if you were living in the wild?" Zoe sighed. Great-Uncle Horace was right, Indie really was brave and curious. She crouched down and stroked Indie's fluffy fur. "Don't worry, there's always something exciting happening here at the Rescue Zoo. I'm sure I'll be able to find something adventurous for you to do. I'll have a think about it while I'm making some Christmas treats for the animals."

As Indie started digging in the snow, Zoe let herself out of the enclosure. A fluffy grey squirrel scampered across her path. He paused for a moment and sat on his hind legs, looking at Zoe as if wondering whether she had any food. But as Zoe opened her mouth to tell him she didn't, he turned and bounded up into the trees in Ruby's enclosure.

Zoe frowned. "Wait a moment. Something's missing, isn't it?"

Meep popped his head out of her hood and they both stared at the gate. The sparkly red bauble Zoe had hung there the day before had disappeared.

"How strange," said Zoe. "What is happening to the decorations?"

Indie came scampering over.

"Indie, did you see anyone take the red bauble from Ruby's gate?" asked Zoe.

The little fox shook her head and yelped.

"You think maybe someone took it down because they didn't like it?" replied Zoe. "But who doesn't like Christmas decorations?" She and Meep looked at each other for a moment and they both exclaimed, "Mr Pinch!"

"He said the red bauble looked messy because it didn't match the silver," said Zoe. "I bet he took the other decorations down too!"

Indie yapped and twitched her whiskers with excitement.

"Indie saw him here last night, shovelling the snow from the footpath," said Zoe. "He didn't see her watching him because she was camouflaged in the snow." She looked at Meep. "I bet he took the bauble because he thought no one was watching." She smiled at Indie through the fence. "Thanks, Indie, we'll be back soon."

"Where are we going?" asked Meep as Zoe strode off along the footpath.

"To see Mr Pinch," she replied. "And hopefully make him give us our baubles back!"

Chapter Four
A Christmas Thief!

Zoe followed the winding footpath to the centre of the zoo. Every so often, as she passed an enclosure, she noticed a gap in the decorations, as if one was missing. When she got to the square at the centre of the zoo, she saw that some long tables had been set up outside the café and gift shop. Lucy and some of the zookeepers

were sitting at the tables, busy wrapping Christmas treats for the animals.

"Hello, Zoe," called Valeria, the keeper from the Rainforest Dome. "Do you want to help me wrap some treats for Sabina?"

"Ooh, yes, please," replied Zoe. Sabina was a sloth who lived in the Rainforest

Dome. Even though she slept most of
the time, she was still a great friend. Zoe
still wanted to find Mr Pinch, but she
couldn't pass up the chance to wrap gifts
first!

"How about wrapping some treats for
Meep?" chirped Meep from inside her
hood.

"Shh!" giggled Zoe. She sat down beside Valeria. There was a selection of Sabina's favourite snacks on the table – flowers, leaves and twigs – and some shiny gold paper to wrap them in. As Zoe began making Sabina her gifts, Alice, the nocturnal mammals' keeper, came over.

"I hear some of your decorations have gone missing too," Alice said to Valeria.

"Yes," replied Valeria. "The silver star on top of the tree outside the dome has disappeared."

Zoe frowned. Surely Mr Pinch wouldn't think the star on top of a Christmas tree was messy? And if he did, wouldn't he tell someone instead of just taking it? He liked things neat and tidy, but he wasn't sneaky.

Just then Mr Pinch came out of the café holding a clipboard. Zoe watched as he made his way along the tables, talking to the zookeepers and writing things down. Finally, he reached their table. Meep quickly dived under Zoe's chair.

"Good morning," said Mr Pinch. "I'm compiling a list of Mysterious Disappearances."

"What do you mean?" asked Zoe.

"I'm trying to solve the mystery of the missing Christmas decorations," he replied.

"So you didn't…" started Zoe.

"Didn't what?" He frowned at her over the top of his clipboard.

"Nothing." Her face flushed. So Mr Pinch definitely hadn't taken the decorations. But if he hadn't, who had?

Mr Pinch sighed. "There's enough mysterious things happening in this zoo without you asking strange questions." He looked along the table. "Has anyone here had a Christmas decoration go missing?"

"Yes!" replied Valeria. "The star from the Rainforest Dome Christmas tree has vanished."

"I've had baubles go missing from

outside the Nocturnal Mammals' House," added Alice.

"And I've had some tinsel taken from outside the animal hospital," said Lucy.

"And someone's taken the red bauble from Ruby's gate," said Zoe. "And the gold ones from outside Indie's."

"Oh dear!" Mr Pinch tutted and sighed as he added the missing decorations to his list. "It would appear that we have a Christmas thief at the zoo!"

As Mr Pinch marched off to the next table, Zoe shivered. This was much more serious than Mr Pinch being fussy and neat. She really didn't like the idea of there being a thief in the zoo! She felt Meep tugging on her trousers under the table.

"What is it?" she whispered, crouching

down. To her surprise, she found Indie
sitting on the ground next to Meep! How
on earth did the little Arctic fox get there?

"Indie," said Zoe, "did you follow us?"
Indie yelped happily to say hello and
nodded her head.

"But how did you get out of your
enclosure?" Zoe asked.

Indie looked at the ground. She didn't want to tell!

"I've got an idea," chirped Meep, interrupting them. "Why don't we make a trap for the thief?"

"What do you mean?"

"We could put up a decoration and wait and see if someone tries to take it?"

"Hmm. But surely no one would steal it if they knew we were watching," replied Zoe.

Indie nudged Zoe's knee with her nose.

"You want to help?" whispered Zoe.

Indie nodded.

Zoe wasn't sure how she felt about Indie escaping her enclosure, but she had promised her an adventure, so she decided it was OK, just this once. She put Meep on her shoulder and stood up, checking that no one had seen the Arctic fox under the table.

"Sorry, Valeria, I just remembered I had to do something. I'll be back soon."

Zoe hurried off along the icy footpath, being careful not to slip. Indie followed after them, camouflaged by the snow.

"What are we doing? Where are we going?" chattered Meep.

"We're going to solve the mystery of the missing decorations *and* give Indie an adventure!" replied Zoe.

Chapter Five
The Missing
Mouse Lemur

As soon as Zoe and Meep had turned the corner, they waited for the Arctic fox to appear.

"Indie!" called Zoe.

At the sound of Zoe's voice, Indie's head popped above the snow a little way behind them. Even though Zoe was worried Mr Pinch would find out that Indie had escaped her enclosure, she couldn't help giggling. Indie was so good at hiding. There was no way Mr Pinch would spot the white fox.

"Come on, let's get you back to your enclosure," said Zoe. "Don't worry, this will be fun!" She gently scooped up the fluffy white animal and carried her the rest of the way.

When Zoe and Meep got to Indie's enclosure, Zoe let the little Arctic fox back in and then searched through her basket of decorations.

"What are you looking for?" asked Meep as he hopped down to the ground.

"This," replied Zoe, pulling out a shiny silver star.

"Now, Indie," said Zoe. "I know how you can help us solve the mystery!"

Indie's blue eyes beamed with joy and she barked.

"It's the mystery of the missing decorations," replied Zoe, and she hung the star on the middle of Indie's fence.

"We think someone has been taking them from around the zoo and we need to find out who it is."

Indie cocked her head to one side, her whiskers twitching as she listened.

"A star just like this has been stolen from the Rainforest Dome," said Zoe. "So I'm going to hang this one here and we'd like you to try and catch the thief."

Indie yelped.

"Because you're so good at camouflaging yourself against the snow," replied Zoe.

Indie shrieked happily and scampered over to the rocks. As soon as she lay down, she blended into the snow.

"It's like you turn invisible," laughed Zoe.

"I wish I was good at camouflaging,"

sighed Meep, his tail drooping.

"You're good at other things," said Zoe, "like eating."

Meep's tail perked a little.

"Thank you, Indie," Zoe called. "We'll come back in the morning to see if you've solved the mystery."

Indie gave a cheery yelp from her hiding place.

The next morning, Zoe woke up as soon as the sun began to rise.

"Come on, Meep, we need to see if Indie has solved the mystery," she said sleepily. But when she looked at Meep's cushion at the end of the bed there was no sign of the little mouse lemur.

Zoe quickly put on a jumper and went downstairs. She could hear a snuffling

sound coming from the kitchen. "Meep?"
She called him softly so she didn't wake
Lucy. "Where are you?" She saw that the
pack of flour had been knocked over and
there was a trail of floury paw-prints
on the counter. Zoe followed
the paw prints to the
windowsill, where she
found Meep covered
from head to toe in
flour.

"What are you
doing?" exclaimed Zoe.
"I was trying to camouflage
myself like Indie," chirped Meep sadly.
"I want to solve the mystery too. But ...
ATISHOO!" he sneezed. "All it's done is
tickle my nose!"

"Oh, Meep," laughed Zoe. "Don't worry, with your fur you'd be great at camouflaging yourself against something grey. Come on, we need to clean up this mess before Mum wakes up."

After they'd cleaned the flour from Meep's fur and the kitchen counter, they set off for Indie's enclosure.

Outside, there was even more snow than before and the rising sun was making it shimmer like gold.

"Look!" squeaked Meep as he raced ahead. "The star has gone!"

Zoe quickly checked the ground to make sure the star hadn't fallen off in the night, but Meep was right. It had disappeared!

"Where's Indie?" chirped Meep, peering through the fence.

Zoe let herself into the enclosure with her paw-shaped pendant and looked around. "Indie, where are you?"

There was movement from the snow-covered rocks and Indie appeared. But instead of scampering over to them like she normally did, she came down really slowly.

"Why is she walking like Sabina the sloth?" asked Meep.

"I don't know." Zoe frowned. "Are you OK, Indie?"

The little Arctic fox gave a sad yelp.

"She didn't see who took the star," Zoe explained to Meep. She bent down and patted Indie on the head. "Don't worry, it doesn't matter."

Indie looked at the fence of her enclosure, where her friend the magpie was perched.

"Did you see anything strange last night?" asked Zoe.

The magpie flew away and Indie made a sad hissing sound.

"It doesn't matter that you fell asleep," replied Zoe. She hated seeing the little Arctic fox look so sad. "Is something wrong?" she asked. Maybe Indie was disappointed that she didn't get to have an adventure. But before Indie could answer, Ethan came hurrying over.

"Hello, Zoe," he called. "You're up bright and early. Mr Pinch has called a meeting in the café before the zoo opens."

"What about?" asked Zoe.

"I don't know," replied Ethan. "He said he had something urgent to discuss. I've got to go and tell the other keepers. I'll see you there."

"Maybe he's discovered who's been taking the decorations," said Zoe as Ethan raced off.

Indie gave a little whimper and ran off to the rocks, where she disappeared inside her burrow.

"Indie seems really sad," chattered Meep as they set off for the café.

"I know," said Zoe. "I guess watching a decoration for hours wasn't a very exciting adventure."

"Yes, no wonder she fell asleep!" chirped Meep.

"I bet she feels really bad for not seeing who took the star," said Zoe. "We need to think of something really special and fun for her to do today."

"Can I do something special and fun too?" chirped Meep as he clambered up on to Zoe's shoulder.

"Wasn't trying to camouflage yourself with flour enough fun for you?" giggled Zoe.

"That wasn't fun at all, it made me sneeze." Meep sniffed.

"All right, I'll see if I can think of something," said Zoe, and they hurried on their way.

Chapter Six
An Urgent Meeting

By the time Zoe and Meep got to the
café it was already full of people. But
instead of being full of visitors, it was full
of zookeepers.

"Hello, Zoe," called Sally, the café
manager. "Would you like a hot
chocolate?"

"Yes, please," replied Zoe.

"What about me, what about me?" squeaked Meep, waving his paws up and down.

"Goodness, Meep seems very excited today," laughed Sally. "Would he like some breakfast?"

"Yes, please," replied Zoe.

Meep's tail bounced up and down as Sally put a bowl of fruit and nuts on the floor in front of him. Zoe felt as excited as Meep, as she watched Sally sprinkle her creamy hot chocolate with delicious marshmallows.

"Zoe, there you are," said Lucy as she entered the cafe. "Sally, could I have a hot chocolate too? I didn't have a chance to eat breakfast. I was going to make pancakes this morning but there wasn't enough flour!" She shook her head. "I was sure we had nearly a full bag."

Meep gave a little squeak of alarm.

"Oh, I knocked it over, sorry," Zoe fibbed. Thankfully her mum wasn't cross and Zoe and Meep exchanged relieved grins.

As they took their drinks over to a table, the café door opened and Great-Uncle Horace walked in. He was wrapped up warm in a long winter coat and a fluffy red scarf.

"Good morning, Zoe. Good morning, Lucy," he said, sitting down beside them.

"Good morning, Great-Uncle Horace," replied Zoe. "Do you know why Mr Pinch has called this meeting?"

"I don't." He shook his head. "It's a mystery."

"Another one," giggled Zoe.

"Yes, the zoo seems full of mysteries this Christmas!" said Lucy.

Finally, Mr Pinch arrived, looking as smart as always in his zoo manager's uniform. He marched up to the counter and coughed loudly to get everyone's attention.

"Hello everyone," he said.

"Hello, Mr Pinch," everyone replied.

"Good morning, Mr Neat and Tidy," chirped Meep, and Zoe had to have a quick sip of hot chocolate to stop herself from giggling.

"I have called you all here today because we need to solve a messy mystery," said Mr Pinch.

"What messy mystery?" called Valeria.

"The messy mystery of the missing decorations, of course," snapped Mr Pinch.

Zoe frowned. "I thought you said the decorations were making the zoo look untidy," she called.

"Yes, but the zoo looks even more

untidy with so many decorations missing," replied Mr Pinch. "At least before they were in neat rows. Now there are gaps all over the place. Even on top of one of the trees." He sighed. "We have our special Christmas event tomorrow and lots of people will be coming to visit the zoo. We need to find the missing decorations and we mustn't lose any more."

"Do you think one of the animals might have taken them?" asked Jane, the kangaroos' keeper.

"I don't see how," said Mr Pinch. "All of the animals are in enclosures. Well, most of them…" He frowned at Meep, who was sitting on the floor eating his berries.

"Meep isn't the thief," said Zoe

indignantly. "I'm with him all the time."
She couldn't help thinking of Indie and
her little escape the other day though.
Zoe still didn't understand how she'd
done it!

"Hmm." Mr Pinch turned his frown on
Zoe.

"I didn't take them!" exclaimed Zoe.

"What if it was one of the zoo visitors?"
suggested Tony, the zebras' keeper.

Mr Pinch shook his head. "Some of the
decorations have gone missing at night,
when the zoo is shut."

"I want all of you to keep your eyes
peeled today," said Mr Pinch. "The thief
needs to be caught."

Zoe crouched down next to Meep.
"We have to solve this mystery," she
whispered. "Once and for all!"

Outside, heavy grey clouds were gathering in the sky. Zoe had thought and thought about how to catch the thief and had come up with nothing. She thought that maybe if she did something different for a while, an idea would come to her.

"It's a shame I can't fly," said Meep.

"Why?" asked Zoe.

"Because then I could camouflage myself against those grey clouds and Mr Pinch wouldn't be able to see me."

Zoe laughed. She couldn't help wishing that she could make herself invisible whenever Mr Pinch was around too! Up ahead of them on the footpath she saw the squirrel from the day before burying a nut in the roots of a big oak tree. *Perhaps he might have seen something*, Zoe thought. But before Zoe had a chance to ask him, he'd scurried up into the tree.

"I've got a brilliant idea!" she exclaimed.

"About how to find the thief?" asked Meep.

"No, about how to give Indie a proper adventure!"

Chapter Seven
The Fastest Treasure Hunt Ever

"The enrichment store is my favourite place in the whole zoo!" Meep chirped happily from Zoe's shoulder. "Or my second favourite, after the food cupboard."

Zoe grinned as she looked around the storeroom. All of the walls were lined with shelves full of fun enrichment toys for the animals. There were balls to bounce, boxes to hide in, squeaky toys, chewy snacks, jingly bells and pieces of rope to pull on. She could see why Meep liked it so much. It was like being in a toy shop for animals!

"Right, we need to fill this," she said, placing her basket on the floor. She'd taken the Christmas decorations out and left them at the cottage.

Meep leapt from her shoulder on to a shelf full of bouncy balls. He threw one down at the basket and it bounced up and hit a box of bells. The bells jingled as the box wobbled on the shelf.

Zoe dived to steady it. "Careful!" she giggled.

"Sorry." Meep hopped on to a shelf containing squeaky toy mice in different colours. He popped a white one into the basket. "Do you think Indie will enjoy this adventure?"

"I hope so," replied Zoe. "I think going on a treasure hunt is a really fun adventure."

"Especially when the treasure is food," said Meep, looking longingly at a shelf full of fruity chew sticks.

Zoe took two down, put one in the basket and gave the other to Meep. "For being such a good helper," she said.

Pretty soon the basket was full. Zoe covered the top with her scarf. "So Indie won't see what we've got," she explained to Meep.

"But how will we bury them without her seeing?" asked Meep.

"We'll have to find something to

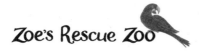

distract her."

Zoe picked up Meep and tucked him
into her coat pocket, then let herself
out of the storeroom using her paw-
print pendant. As they set off along the
winding footpath through the zoo, the
fences of the enclosures glimmered and

sparkled with beautiful decorations. But for once Zoe couldn't help agreeing with Mr Pinch. It did look a bit strange with all the gaps from the decorations that were missing. Maybe giving Indie an adventure would help her come up with an idea to catch the thief.

When they reached Indie's enclosure, Zoe spotted the magpie sitting in one of the trees by the gate.

"Hello," whispered Zoe to the bird. "Can you come down here?"

The bird tweeted and fluttered down, landing on top of the gate. He puffed up his black and white feathers and cocked his head to one side.

"We need you to help us," said Zoe, looking around to make sure Indie wasn't anywhere nearby. "We've got a surprise planned for Indie. Please can you distract her while we get it ready?"

The bird started chattering happily and flew off to the top of the rocks, where Indie suddenly appeared.

"Phew!" exclaimed Zoe. "Now that they're playing together we'll be able to hide the treasure." She took Meep out of her pocket and set him down on the ground. One by one they took the toys from the basket and began burying them in the snow. Zoe kept checking to make sure Indie wasn't watching. The magpie was trying to keep the little fox distracted, swooping around her and playfully pecking at her tail. But Indie wasn't being her normal playful self. She was standing still and flicking her tail half-heartedly. Zoe frowned as she wondered what was wrong. Hopefully the treasure hunt would cheer Indie up.

Just as Zoe buried the last of the toys,
Indie noticed them and came scampering
over. As Zoe bent down to greet her, she
yelped.

"We've made an adventure for you,"
explained Zoe. "We've buried treasure
all over your enclosure for you to find."

Indie's whiskers twitched and she sniffed the air, then began to dig. She found the first toy within seconds. Then she found another and another. As she raced around the enclosure burrowing in the snow and uncovering the treasure, Meep waved his paws in the air.

"This is going to be the shortest treasure hunt ever!" he chattered.

Indie came scampering over with the fruity stick in her mouth.

"Well done!" exclaimed Zoe. "You found them all so quickly."

Indie barked proudly.

"She says that Arctic foxes have really powerful noses," explained Zoe to Meep. "She was able to smell them under the snow."

"Mouse lemurs have powerful noses too," said Meep, puffing up his chest. "Especially when it comes to food."

"I know!" giggled Zoe. She patted Indie on the head. "I'm sorry your adventure was over so soon."

Indie yelped.

"Oh dear," said Zoe.

"What's wrong?" asked Meep.

"She says she really enjoyed the treasure hunt, but it wasn't an adventure." Zoe stroked Indie's fluffy fur. "Why wasn't it an adventure?" she asked the little Arctic fox.

Indie put her head to one side and yelped again.

"An adventure needs to be important and unplanned," repeated Zoe. "I see. Well, that is a little more difficult."

Indie picked up the toy mouse with her mouth and it gave a loud squeak.

"I'm glad you enjoyed finding your new toys though," said Zoe. "I don't suppose you've seen anyone acting suspiciously around the decorations?"

Indie dropped the mouse and her tail drooped. She shook her fluffy white head, looking really sad. Overhead in the trees, the squirrel leapt from branch to branch.

"Don't worry," said Zoe.

Watching Indie trot off to the rocks, Zoe felt guilty. She'd tried so hard to cheer up the little Arctic fox but now she'd upset her again. She picked up her empty basket and put Meep inside it.

"I feel really bad for upsetting Indie," she said as they left the enclosure. "Now we have two important missions."

"Is one of them to get me some food?" asked Meep hopefully.

"No!" replied Zoe. "One is to solve the mystery of the missing decorations, and the other is to find Indie a proper adventure and cheer her up."

Chapter Eight
Another Mystery!

The next day Zoe was woken by the sound of Meep chattering excitedly. She opened her eyes and saw that he was standing on her bedroom windowsill.

"What are you doing?" she murmured sleepily.

"The whole world has turned white!" chattered the little mouse lemur.

"Really?" Zoe went to the end of her bed and looked out of the window. "Wow!" she exclaimed.

It had snowed a lot more in the night and everything was white. She looked down into the cottage garden. The snow came halfway up the gate.

"It's so deep!" exclaimed Zoe. "I hope the visitors will still be able to come to the zoo for the Christmas celebration, and that we'll be able to give the animals their Christmas treats."

"I hope so too!" chirped Meep, looking really worried.

"It's OK. You'll definitely be getting your treat." Zoe picked him up and gave him a cuddle. "Come on, let's go and see what Mum thinks."

Downstairs in the kitchen, Lucy was

taking a tray of freshly baked Christmas cookies from the oven. Meep licked his lips.

"Morning, love," said Lucy, coming over to give Zoe a hug.

"Morning, Mum. Have you seen how deep the snow is? Do you think the zoo will be able to open?"

"I hope so," replied Lucy, handing Zoe a freshly baked cookie and a glass of milk. Meep chirped loudly and Lucy peeled a banana and handed it to him. Just then there was a knock on the door. Zoe opened it to find Great-Uncle Horace standing in the snow dressed as Santa. His cheeks were as red as his coat from the cold.

"Ho, ho, ho!" he boomed. "Or should it be snow, snow, snow!" he chuckled.

Kiki flew down from his shoulder, flapping the snow from her wings.

"It's so deep," said Zoe. "Will people still be able to visit the zoo?"

"Don't worry, I've just heard that the roads have been cleared," replied Great-Uncle Horace. "All we have to do is clear the footpaths."

Zoe quickly got changed into some warm clothes and boots. Then she tucked Meep inside her coat pocket and they all followed Great-Uncle Horace through the zoo. The snow was so deep in some places it came to the top of Zoe's boots! All of the zookeepers had gathered by the zoo café, where Mr Pinch was handing out spades.

"Make sure you dig in neat lines," he called. "I'll be checking to make sure your digging is straight."

"I'm having trouble finding the entrance to the giraffes' enclosure," said Theo, the giraffes' keeper.

"Same here," said Valeria. "The snow is so deep outside the Rainforest Dome."

"But if we can't get to the enclosures, we won't be able to give the animals their Christmas treats," said Zoe.

"Maybe we'll have to leave it," said Mr Pinch.

Meep gave a sad little whimper from Zoe's coat pocket.

"Don't worry," whispered Zoe, stroking him on the head. "There must be some way we can burrow our way through the snow." Her face lit up. "I've got a great idea!" she cried.

"What is it?" asked Great-Uncle Horace.

"Why don't we get Indie to help us? She loves the snow and she loves to burrow. She could show us where to dig."

"That's an excellent idea, Zoe," said Ethan.

The other keepers all nodded in agreement.

"But will she burrow in a straight line?" muttered Mr Pinch.

"Let's go and dig her out," said Great-Uncle Horace.

They all set off to Indie's enclosure, where they began digging through the snow. The magpie fluttered above them, chattering a song, and soon they'd made a tunnel to the gate.

Zoe let herself into the enclosure and ran over to Indie.

"We need your help," she whispered as the little Arctic fox nuzzled up against her. "The animals are all snowed into their enclosures and we can't find the entrances. Will you burrow through the snow to the gates so we can give them their treats?"

Indie yelped excitedly and Zoe gave a

sigh of relief. It was great to see the little
Arctic fox looking happy again.

When they got back to the café, Zoe noticed that some of the zookeepers were frowning.

"What's happened?" she asked Alice.

"Now some of the Christmas treats for the animals have gone missing," replied Alice.

"It's really strange," said Valeria. "It's only the ones wrapped in gold paper."

"The thief strikes again," said Mr Pinch.

Zoe's heart sank. "This is really bad," she muttered to Indie and Meep. "The visitors will be here any minute. We don't have time to make any more. Some of the animals won't get their treats."

Indie's head dropped and she gave a sad hissing sound.

"What's wrong?" asked Zoe, crouching down next to her.

Indie yelped.

"You know who took the decorations?" exclaimed Zoe.

"Who is it?" Meep chirped.

Indie hissed quietly.

"The magpie!" exclaimed Zoe. She was really shocked. The magpie was such a friendly, cheery bird. Why would it have stolen so many decorations? But then she remembered learning about magpies in school. Her teacher had said that magpies liked putting sparkly things in their nests. "You saw him taking the silver star?" Zoe said to Indie.

Indie nodded.

"But why didn't she tell us before?" asked Meep.

"Because the magpie is her friend and she didn't want to get him into trouble," replied Zoe. "I bet he took the treats as well as the decorations. Magpies love shiny things."

While the adults were still busy discussing what to do about the Christmas treats, Zoe, Meep and Indie slipped back into her enclosure.

"Don't worry," Zoe said to Indie. "I won't tell the magpie you told me. Just show me where I can find him."

Indie led her over to a tree at the back of her enclosure. As Zoe stared up into the branches, she caught a glimpse of something silver.

"Hello," called Zoe. The magpie appeared from its nest and gave her a cheery cheep. "I'm just checking all over the zoo for some missing decorations," explained Zoe. "I don't suppose you've seen any?"

The bird fluttered his wings nervously.

"Don't worry, you're not in trouble," called Zoe. "It's just that we need them back for our Christmas celebrations."

The magpie swooped down through the branches with the silver star and a pass-card in his beak. He placed them on the ground in front of Zoe and cawed sadly.

"It's OK," said Zoe. "I like shiny things too. I promise I'll get you something shiny for your nest as a Christmas treat.

And you got the card from one of the zookeepers so that Indie could go out and explore? That's very sweet of you – but Indie is much safer inside her enclosure!"

The magpie cawed again.

"You didn't think that taking just one decoration would be a problem?" said Zoe. "Wait, is this star the only thing you took?"

The magpie nodded his head.

Zoe frowned. "But then who took the other decorations?"

Meep sighed and shook his head. "Looks like we've got another mystery!"

Chapter Nine
Indie to the Rescue

Zoe looked around the snow-covered enclosure. If the magpie hadn't taken the other decorations, who could it have been? She turned to ask Indie what she thought, but found that the little Arctic fox had disappeared again!

"Indie!" called Zoe. She heard a rustling from outside the enclosure and out popped the Arctic fox's fluffy white head.

Indie yelped and her head disappeared again. "You think you might have solved the mystery?" asked Zoe with a grin. She ran out of the enclosure with Meep still tucked in her pocket to where Indie had last appeared.

There was a scuffling sound and then Indie jumped out of a hole near a big oak tree, with something clasped in her mouth. A glittery gold bauble!

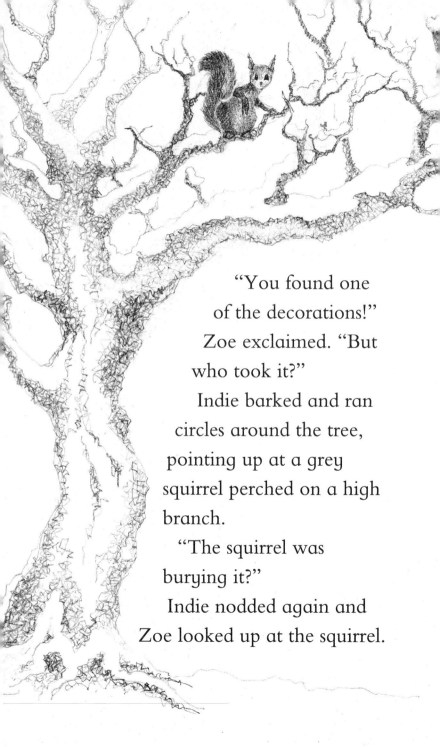

"You found one
of the decorations!"
Zoe exclaimed. "But
who took it?"

Indie barked and ran
circles around the tree,
pointing up at a grey
squirrel perched on a high
branch.

"The squirrel was
burying it?"

Indie nodded again and
Zoe looked up at the squirrel.

"I don't suppose you've seen any other Christmas decorations?" Zoe called to him.

The squirrel's tail drooped. He looked really embarrassed.

"You're not in any trouble," said Zoe. "We just need them back for our Christmas celebrations."

The squirrel squeaked sadly.

"You were sad that everyone in the zoo got pretty things except you?" Zoe repeated. She looked at the squirrel again. "Did you take some little parcels wrapped in gold too?"

The squirrel nodded.

"They were Christmas treats for the animals," explained Zoe. The squirrel looked so sad that she felt really sorry for him. "Don't worry, if you give us our decorations and treats back, I promise to get something lovely and shiny just for you."

The squirrel gave a cheery squeak but then his tail drooped again.

"You don't remember where you buried them all?" Zoe's heart sank. How would they find the missing treats now?

As Zoe thought about what they could do, Indie started sniffing at the bauble she'd found, before she disappeared into the new burrow.

"Maybe we won't find them after all, Meep." Zoe sighed. What would they give the animals now?

"Look! Look!" Meep chattered. Just as Zoe turned away, Indie had jumped out of the snow and there was a flash of gold in her mouth!

Zoe and Meep watched as Indie scampered in and out of the fresh burrow she'd made, leaving a pile of decorations and treats wrapped in gold at their feet. There were all of the missing things. Indie had saved the day!

Once all of the decorations and treats had been uncovered, Zoe took them back to the café with Meep and Indie scampering after her.

"Indie found them buried in the ground," she told everyone. "I think a squirrel had been putting them there."

"Great work, Indie!" said Great-Uncle Horace, patting her on the head. All of the keepers clapped and cheered.

As soon as everyone had got their treats and decorations back, Zoe took Indie to Ruby's enclosure. Indie set to work burrowing a tunnel to the entrance. Ruby watched from up in a tree and the magpie circled above them. Meep was perched on top of Zoe's spade. They waited and waited but there was no sign of the little Arctic fox.

"Shouldn't she have got to the gate by now?" chirped Meep.

"Yes, I hope she's OK," replied Zoe, feeling worried.

There was a loud squeaking noise by the fence and Zoe saw a pair of bright-blue eyes blinking out from the snow. "Indie, sometimes you're too well camouflaged," she giggled. As she started digging her way over, Zoe heard a startled yelp. She looked up to see that one of the banks of snow Indie had burrowed through had fallen in.

"Indie!" yelled Zoe.

"What's wrong?" asked Meep.

"The tunnel she dug has collapsed on top of her!" exclaimed Zoe.

The magpie swooped down, squawking

and flapping its wings frantically.

"Maybe she's just camouflaged," said Meep.

"No, she's buried," replied Zoe. She began digging frantically at the snow.

All of a sudden, some whiskers appeared, followed by a pointy nose and Indie's smiling face came bursting out.

"Indie! Are you OK?" Zoe gasped.

Indie squeaked happily.

"I'm very glad you had an adventure," said Zoe. "I just wish it hadn't been quite so scary!" She took the bright-red bauble down from Ruby's gate.

"What are you doing?" chirped Meep. "We only just put that back up."

"It's OK," replied Zoe. "I'm taking it down for a very important reason." She tied the bauble to Indie's tail. "It's so we don't lose you in all this snow," she explained.

Indie yelped gleefully and wagged her tail. High above her the magpie swooped and soared and sang a cheery song.

Once Indie had burrowed her way to every enclosure entrance, Zoe took her and Meep to the zoo café. The tables outside were filled with zoo visitors wrapped up warmly and drinking hot chocolate.

Ethan was standing by the signpost in front of the café. When he saw Zoe he smiled and nodded.

Zoe crouched down beside Indie. "There's one more place we'd like you to burrow to," she whispered in her ear, and pointed to the signpost. The little Arctic fox fluffed up her fur and twitched her whiskers and with a yelp she disappeared into the snow. The visitors at the tables all fell silent as they watched and waited.

"I hope she doesn't get buried again," chirped Meep as Zoe took him from her pocket.

"Me too!" agreed Zoe. But just when she was about to get worried, the snow by the signpost began to move and there was a sudden glimmer of red. "There's her bauble!" exclaimed Zoe. Then the rest of Indie appeared. In her mouth was a treat wrapped in gold. "Happy Christmas, Indie!" Zoe cried. "Well done for finding your treat."

As she and Meep hurried over to give Indie a cuddle, Zoe smiled. Life at the zoo had certainly got a lot more exciting since Indie arrived. She wondered if the next animal Great-Uncle Horace rescued would be just as adventurous!

If you enjoyed Indie's story,
look out for:

The Runaway Reindeer

Amelia Cobb

nosy
crow

Chapter One
Christmas Emergency!

Zoe Parker looked at the twinkly lights hanging around the room and gave a happy sigh. Christmas was her favourite holiday, but this year it was going to be even more special. This year, her friend Talia and her mum had come to stay. Talia's mum, Katie, and Zoe's mum, Lucy, had been best friends since they were little.

"Do you think anyone's ever made an advent calendar for a red panda before?" asked Zoe, carefully cutting a door in the front of a large cardboard box. On the floor beside her were a pile of apples, bamboo and pieces of corn bread to hide behind the doors.

"I don't think so," giggled Talia. "Do you think anyone's ever made a monkey a cuddly snowman?" She held up the toy snowman she'd been making.

"Definitely not," laughed Zoe. "But I know the monkeys are going to love it!"

"Spending Christmas in a zoo is the best!" exclaimed Talia as she put the finishing touches to the snowman's face.

Zoe grinned. Thanks to her Great-Uncle Horace, she got to spend every

Christmas in a zoo because she lived in the Rescue Zoo that he owned. Great-Uncle Horace was a famous explorer and animal expert. He'd created the Rescue Zoo as a safe place for animals who were endangered, lost or hurt. Zoe and her mum lived in a cottage in the zoo because Lucy was the zoo vet.

Zoe started painting a robin on the advent calendar door. She had asked her Great-Uncle Horace if she and Talia could come to his house, Higgins Hall, to make some Christmas treats for the zoo animals. The girls were sitting in front of the large fireplace in Great-Uncle Horace's living room. A fire was crackling away in the hearth and paints, cardboard and pieces of fruit covered the rug all around them.

Zoe's mouse lemur, Meep, waved his paws as he looked at the fruit. His long grey tail bobbed up and down with excitement.

"Can I have a treat? Can I have a treat?" he chattered.

"I wonder what Meep's saying," said Talia.

"I wonder." Zoe smiled. The truth was, she knew exactly what Meep was saying because Zoe had a very special secret. Ever since she was six years old, she'd been able to understand animals – and they could understand her too. No one else knew her secret, not even her mum or Great-Uncle Horace. Zoe had to be very careful not to give it away.

"I think he must be getting excited for Christmas," she said. She stroked the little mouse lemur's silky fur. "Don't worry, Meep, it's only three days until Christmas. Santa will come late on Christmas Eve and then you'll have loads of treats in your stocking."

Zoe's Rescue Zoo

Look out for more amazing animal adventures at the Rescue Zoo!

The Rescue Princesses

Look out for
another AMAZING
series from Nosy Crow!

Friendship, animals and
secret royal adventures!